DRAGON GIRLS

Rani the
Enchanted Dragon

Maddy Mara

SPECIAL EDITION

DRAGON GIRLS

Rani the Enchanted Dragon

by Maddy Mara

Scholastic Inc.

ISBN 978-1-5461-2194-7

10 9 8 7 6 5 4 3 2 1   24 25 26 27 28

Printed in the U.S.A.   40

First printing 2024

Book design by Cassy Price

Rani's sister, Anjali, stood in the middle of the stage, her silky dress floating like a cloud around her. Rani was watching from the side of the stage, her heart beating fast. Her family ran the Magic Star Theater, so Rani saw most of the plays over and over. But it didn't matter how many times she saw this one—she never grew tired of it. Anjali was a great actor, for one thing. And for another, Anjali was moving to another city to study acting in a few weeks. Rani was going to miss her, and wanted to spend as much time with her big sister as she could before she left.

Onstage, the golden spotlight made Anjali glow. "The dawn is coming. I must fly!" she said, stretching up her arms. The audience gasped as she leapt into the air and flew—she actually flew!—across the stage.

Rani hugged herself. This scene was so spellbinding. She knew how the flying trick worked, of course. Rani had watched the stage technicians put the harness, attached to wires, on Anjali. But somehow, whenever she saw it onstage, it looked truly magical.

With a little jolt, Rani remembered she had a job to do! She flicked the switch on the

machine next to her. Smoke curled out and billowed across the stage like a cloud. Rani wiggled her fingers, pretending that she had made the cloud with her magic powers. Being able to do spells would be so amazing!

Slowly, the cloud turned pink and orange. This was thanks to Rani's mom, who was in the lighting booth at the back of the theater.

Hidden high above the stage, stagehands scattered tiny pieces of shiny paper, which floated down like shimmering raindrops.

Next came the highlight of the scene, in

Rani's opinion. Anjali floated into the middle of the stage and hovered.

Rani held her breath, waiting.

Anjali clapped her hands and disappeared in a cloud of stars!

Of course, Anjali didn't really disappear. The stunt was a combination of clever lighting and a pulley system.

The audience clapped and cheered loudly as the red curtain fell.

"Well done, everyone!" the director called. "Quick, take your places for final bows!"

The clapping grew steadily louder. Rani watched as the entire cast hurried onto the stage, whispering excitedly to one another. But underneath all the noise, Rani could hear something else. It sounded like singing.

Magic Forest, Magic Forest, come explore…

Rani looked around. Had someone turned a radio on? Was it someone's ringtone? No one else seemed to have heard it. Onstage, Anjali and the other actors held hands as the curtain rose.

The audience roared with delight and Rani joined in. Sometimes, Rani felt a tiny bit jealous of Anjali. She was so talented and got so much attention. But other times, like now, Rani felt so proud of her sister she could burst.

Despite all the applause, Rani heard that strange singing again.

Magic Forest, Magic Forest, come explore…

How odd! The voice seemed to be swirling above her somewhere. *I bet it's Dad,* thought

Rani. *He's probably working on some cool new sound effect.*

A smile twitched on Rani's lips. This might even be a little test her father had set up to see if she could figure out what was going on.

While the audience continued to cheer and clap, Rani snuck into the area behind the stage. She had a feeling this was where her dad would be. It was where all the scenery and props for their plays were stored.

Rani ducked around a cardboard lamppost, a stack of chairs, and a row of wooden trees with fabric leaves. She strained her ears, listening for the song. It seemed to have faded, but excitement buzzed through Rani. It was like the feeling she got on the opening night of a new show.

"Dad? Are you there?" she half whispered.

There was no reply. The noise from the stage seemed very far away. Rani kept going, walking between the fake trees. Her hand brushed against one of them and she yelped. The painted bark felt real—not like a prop at all. And since when had the backstage area gotten so big?

Magic Forest, Magic Forest, come explore...

The singing was louder now. And Rani had the weirdest feeling that it was being sung just for her. Or just to her.

"Who's there?" Rani called. "You know, this area is out of—"

A layer of fog curled around her feet. Oh no! She must have forgotten to turn off the smoke machine! But this smoke was different.

It swirled with colors—aqua, pink, and purple. Also, it smelled of flowers.

Rani's fingers began to tingle. If this was a special effect that her dad had created, it was his best yet. But as the colored smoke continued to build, Rani realized this was not her dad's work.

Something very unusual was going on. When she heard the mysterious song again, Rani felt like the words were already inside her.

Magic Forest, Magic Forest, come explore.
Magic Forest, Magic Forest, hear my roar!

Rani took a step forward. Her pulse was very fast, but she wasn't afraid. She knew she was being called upon to play an important role. But not a role on the stage, like her sister. Something bigger, and maybe a little dangerous.

"I'll gladly come and explore," she called into the darkness. "Just show me the way."

A single beam of light fell from above, lighting up a spot on the floor. Rani stepped onto it. The fog curled tightly around her like a blanket. She was surrounded by streaks of swirling color. Then came a burst of stars!

Rani closed her eyes against the brightness as the floor dissolved beneath her feet.

Even without opening her eyes, Rani knew she was no longer backstage. She could feel it! The air smelled like a lush garden on a summer's night. A gentle breeze tickled her face, and she could hear the sound of rustling leaves.

Rani opened her eyes and looked around. She was in a forest at twilight! Could this possibly be real? Rani had always hoped something magical would happen to her. Had it finally? But Rani had grown up in the theater, so she knew this could all be a fancy set. The trees and grass might be props. The breeze could be a wind machine, the chirping insects the work of a sound artist.

Rani looked up. Overhead, ripples of color moved against a darkening sky. As she watched, the colors split apart and danced away.

If this was done by a lighting expert, then they were very talented!

I'm going to explore, Rani decided. But after a couple of steps, she stopped. What was going on with her body? It felt different. Like, *really* different. She glanced down and nearly fell over in surprise.

Her sneakered feet had become massive paws, each with a set of curved talons. And

her legs were covered in gleaming scales...
and so was the rest of her body! Looking
over her shoulder, Rani saw a tail dragging
behind her. Best of all, on her back was a pair
of powerful wings.

"I've turned into a dragon!" Rani said. She
shook her head, feeling dazed. "No, that's
impossible. I must be in a costume. And this
place can't be real."

From a nearby bush came a whispered con-
versation. "Did you hear that? The Dragon Girl
doesn't believe she's a dragon!"

"And she doesn't think the Magic Forest is
real! Even though she's standing right in the
middle of it!"

"I wonder if that happens with all Dragon
Girls when they first arrive?"

Rani froze. Maybe there were dangerous

animals lurking? She shook the thought away. Animals couldn't talk. Besides, the voices sounded friendly.

Rani knelt down—a little awkwardly in her powerful dragon form—in front of the rustling bush. "Hello!" she said. "Who's in there?"

Rani heard frantic whispers. "She heard us!"

"We're going to be in soooooo much trouble!"

"Quick! Let's go before she sees us."

Very carefully, Rani reached out and parted the bushes. Three tiny creatures tumbled onto the grass. Rani stared at them. She had never seen animals like them.

The first one looked like a very small, very fuzzy lion cub with big green eyes. On her back sprouted a pair of blue-and-green butterfly wings. She growled in surprise as she rolled to a stop.

The second one was a pale blue puppy with flecks of gold through her fur. She also had wings. Her bright blue eyes were fixed on Rani.

The final creature looked like some kind of penguin, except that she was purple and her webbed feet (which were currently waggling in the air) and eyes were gold.

"Hello! What kind of creatures are you?"

Rani asked softly, not wanting to scare them away. She'd never seen anything so cute in her life!

"We're Questies," said the butterfly-lion cub in a soft, purry voice. "My name is Flittercub."

"Questies is short for Quest Friends," explained the puppy, wagging her tail and flapping her wings all at once. "Our job is to help Dragon Girls on their quests in the Magic Forest. I'm TrustyPup, by the way."

"And I'm Splishi," the tiny penguin said, finally righting herself and standing up. "Also, we're not *big* Questies yet. We're just juniors. But we'll be real Questies one day. We just need everything to go back to normal so we can finish our training."

"That's why we are SO excited you're here!" Flittercub purred. "There are some big problems in the Magic Forest right now. You'll fix them for us, right? That's what Dragon Girls do, after all."

"Umm..." Rani had no idea what to say. How could she fix anything? Her brain was still struggling to accept that she was a Dragon Girl, whatever that meant.

It was funny. Whenever Rani couldn't sleep

at night or concentrate at school, magic was what she daydreamed about. But now that something magical was definitely happening, Rani wasn't sure how she felt about it.

TrustyPup gave a little bark. "Where are the other two Dragon Girls?" She looked around. "There are always three, aren't there?"

"Maybe things are different this time," Splishi suggested, scratching her beak with a wing. "The whole forest is topsy-turvy."

Rani felt like she'd been dropped onstage halfway through a play. She had no idea what was going on.

"What are the problems?" she asked finally. That felt like an important first thing to understand.

The creatures' eyes widened nervously. "There's bad magic in the air," Flittercub whispered. "It's like the forest has been put under a spell."

"And all the trained Questies have disappeared," TrustyPup added, her tail drooping. "Including my big brother." She gave a sad little howl.

"Plus, the forest is full of weird, scary lights," Splishi said in her high voice.

"You mean the ones up in the sky?" Rani asked. She was surprised. The colorful swirls had looked beautiful to her, not scary.

"No, those are Sky Swirls," Flittercub said. "They're good."

"The swirls come every year," Splishi explained. "They get bigger and brighter for a few days, then they rain their colorful magic over the forest."

"This gives all the plants and creatures their

magical power," Splishi said. "The Sky Swirls are very important."

"But this year, they're not getting brighter." Flittercub growled softly. "In fact, they're already fading."

Rani tilted her head. "So what are the weird, scary lights you mentioned?"

"We don't know. They move through the forest like shadows," TrustyPup said.

"But they are bright and glowing," Splishi added with a shudder. "We don't trust them at all!"

Rani could understand why. A bright, glowing shadow sounded all wrong. Right then, Rani made a decision. She had no idea what was going on, but it was clear that these adorable creatures needed her help. The only problem was where should she start?

"You must go to the glade," Splishi said suddenly.

Rani stared at her in surprise. "Did you read my mind?"

"Not exactly," Splishi said. "But Questies are good at sensing what Dragon Girls are thinking and feeling. The more time they spend together, the better they get."

"Shows that we are natural Questies!" Flittercub said proudly. She turned to Rani. "You must go to the glade," she explained. "That's where the Tree Queen lives. She'll tell you what to do."

The Tree Queen! Rani felt a ripple of excitement. This Magic Forest was getting more and more interesting. She tried to imagine what a Tree Queen would look like. And what would she say?

Flittercub did a loop in the air. It was slightly wonky but still impressive. "Have you ever flown before, Dragon Girl?" she asked.

"Not really," Rani said. She had tried out the

harness with wires at the theater. But that probably didn't count as real flying.

"Go on, then—give it a try!" Splishi flapped her own little wings furiously, rising off the ground.

The three Questies looked expectantly at Rani.

Feeling like she was in a dream, Rani gave her huge wings a flap. Nothing happened. She tried again. Still nothing. Her wings were surprisingly heavy. Flapping them took a lot of strength.

"Don't give up, Dragon Girl!" Splishi called. "Flying was hard for us at the start, too." As if to prove this, Splishi suddenly plummeted downward, just managing to stop before she hit the earth.

I can do this, Rani told herself as the other two Questies copied Splishi, taking turns at diving toward the ground and stopping at the last moment. *Maybe I need to pretend I'm in the flying harness at the theater?*

Rani pictured herself onstage, slipping on the harness. She imagined the long wires attached to the harness lifting her up.

This time when she flapped her wings, she rose smoothly into the air.

A huge smile stretched across Rani's face. Zooming across the stage in a harness was very fun. But it was nothing like this! She felt all her muscles working as she flew to the top of the tall trees. The leaves rustled wildly as she flapped. Her wings were so powerful!

For a moment she hovered in place, looking around the forest. It was beautiful, bathed in

the light of early evening. Then, pressing her wings against her body, Rani dove toward the ground. She felt like a comet streaking through the sky. As she neared the ground, she swerved high again.

The Questies flew up to meet her. "Flying's the best, isn't it?" Flittercub said.

"But it's also really hard," TrustyPup said. "Especially in a group."

"Group flying isn't hard," Splishi said, just as she crashed into the other two. The three little creatures tumbled down onto the soft grass. They jumped to their feet and flew back into the air.

Rani got the feeling it wasn't the first time this had happened.

"So, should we go and meet this Tree Queen?" Rani was feeling a little nervous. She had never met a queen before—especially not one who was also a tree! "Can you lead me there?"

The three creatures exchanged a look.

"You *do* know the way, don't you?" Rani asked.

"I have no idea!" Splishi admitted cheerfully.

"I am pretty sure it's that way," Flittercub said, pointing a paw.

"I went past the glade once with my brother PlushyPup," TrustyPup said. "But I was only little then."

Rani fought back a laugh. It was hard to imagine TrustyPup being any smaller than she already was.

"Well, I'm sure we'll figure it out together," Rani said, trying to sound more confident than she felt. "Come on, everyone. Let's go!"

Flapping her wings strongly, Rani began flying in the direction Flittercub had pointed. The Questies hurried to overtake her so they could lead.

Rani could hear them whispering.

"Are you sure this is the right way?"

"I'm sort of sure."

"We can't get the Dragon Girl lost. That would be bad."

Back home, Rani was always the youngest and the smallest. The one everyone else protected. But here, she suddenly felt like the big, responsible one.

"You three are doing great," Rani called. "You'll get me there, I know it."

She just hoped this turned out to be true!

As she grew more confident flying, Rani started to look around. The sun had now fully set, but the forest was far from dark. The swirling colors overhead illuminated everything in soft pinks, greens, and oranges. Down below, Rani saw little bell-shaped flowers that glowed like fairy lights.

Something caught her eye. Deep within the thick trees ahead, Rani saw a strange shape.

It was flat like a silhouette but made of light. It was very bright but also seemed cold somehow. A bad feeling gripped Rani's chest. There

was something dangerous about that light. She watched it moving through the forest, sliding over the grass and across fallen leaves. Everything it touched instantly curled up or withered away.

What would happen if it touched an animal?

"Watch out!" squeaked the Questies, banging into one another in their panic. "It's a Bright Shadow!"

Every instinct in Rani's body told her to fly away as quickly as she could. But then she would never get to the glade. She also hated seeing the Questies so scared. Fighting that instinct, Rani instead lunged toward the strange, glowing shadow.

"Go away!" Her voice sounded very loud. In fact, it was a roar! It echoed through the forest. The Bright Shadow stopped, then slipped off the way it had come, leaving a burned trail behind it.

The Questies whooped and looped through the air. "You did it, Dragon Girl!"

Once again, their wings got tangled up and they tumbled to the ground.

Laughing, Rani swooped down to help them up. "Come on, you three. We have a glade to find, remember?"

"Actually, I think we've found it!" TrustyPup said, pointing with her paw to a gap in the trees.

Rani saw a clearing, protected by a wall of shimmering air. It looked like the heat rising from the pavement on a hot day. As they got closer, Rani saw the outline of trees and flowers.

"That's definitely the Tree Queen's glade!"

TrustyPup said, clapping her paws. "I remember seeing that force field when PlushyPup and I went past."

"See? I told you we'd find it," Splishi said.

Rani chose not to remind Splishi that she'd said nothing like that!

"Go on, Dragon Girl. You can fly through that force field." Flittercub gave Rani a friendly nudge with her nose. "But you must go through alone."

"The Tree Queen will be waiting for you," TrustyPup added.

"So I guess this is goodbye?" Rani had known these tiny animals for only a short time, but she was already very fond of them.

"Yes," TrustyPup said, a little sadly. "For now, at least."

"I am sure we'll meet again," Splishi added,

trying to wrap her flippers around Rani's much-too-big neck.

With a lump in her throat, Rani looked at the glistening air. She really hoped the force field didn't burn the way that the Bright Shadow did.

I just have to trust that these little folks know what's safe, she told herself. Taking a deep breath, Rani flew through the twinkling barrier.

To her relief, the force field didn't burn at all! She only felt a slight tingling against her scales, like the buzz of an electric toothbrush on her teeth. Rani blinked as she landed on a patch of soft grass. The light was brighter inside the glade. It felt like a warm afternoon, with birds and glittering insects flying around.

Growing in the very center of the glade was a tall tree. Rani stared at it curiously. Was this

the Tree Queen? It was certainly impressive,

but it didn't look anything like a queen.

The tree's branches began to sway, gently at

first, then with more force. As Rani watched in amazement, the tree slowly turned into a woman. She had long, glossy hair, a shiny green gown, warm brown eyes, and a dazzling smile.

"You must be the Tree Queen!" Rani cried. Then she wondered if it was okay to speak to a queen like this. Especially one who was also a tree.

"You made it!" the Tree Queen said, in a voice that was regal yet somehow earthy. "I wasn't sure if you would find your way here. Normally a Quest Friend leads the Dragon Girls to me." The Tree Queen gave a sigh like a small gust of wind. "But there are no trained Questies right now. That's one of the reasons the Magic Forest needs your help."

"Oh, but three Questies did lead me here," Rani said. "Flittercub, TrustyPup, and Splishi."

The Tree Queen gave a laugh of surprise.

"They did? How wonderful! Those three have only just begun their training. It generally takes many moons before a Quest Friend is experienced enough to guide a Dragon Girl to me."

"They are little, but they did a very good job," Rani said. She decided not to mention all the crashes and near-misses along the way.

"I am so glad, Enchanted Dragon," the Tree Queen said.

"*Enchanted* Dragon?" Rani repeated. "Is that what I am? Does that mean I can do spells?"

"You have many powers, as you will find out in time." The Tree Queen smiled, her wood-brown eyes twinkling. Then her expression became serious. "I have something very important to ask of you. In fact, it's a quest. It won't be easy. And normally, you would have two other Dragon Girls to assist you, as well as a fully trained Quest Friend. But things are far from normal in the Magic Forest right now. That's why we so desperately need your help. It's also why this is the most difficult quest I have ever asked of a Dragon Girl. So tell me, will you accept the challenge?"

That was easy to answer. Of course Rani would accept!

Rani wanted to hear all about the quest, but first she needed to know more about what it meant to be a Dragon Girl. "Are there other ordinary girls like me who turn into dragons when they arrive here?"

The Tree Queen nodded, her leaves rustling. "There are many others. But these girls are far from ordinary. Like you, they are vital to the safety and harmony of the Magic Forest. This place is very old and very precious. It is so vast that I cannot possibly protect it on my own. I am very lucky to have Dragon Girls I can call upon to assist me."

Rani nodded, eager to hear more. She loved the idea that she was one of many Dragon Girls. Maybe she had even met some of them back home, without realizing.

"There has always been a strong connection between your home and this forest," the Tree Queen continued, swaying a little. "Certain girls have dragon powers they don't know about. Once they enter the Magic Forest, those powers awaken. Often they are strongest when they work with other Dragon Girls."

Rani let this sink in. "Then why am I the only one here this time?"

"There is toxic magic in the forest right now. This has weakened the connection between your home and ours," the queen explained. "I feared that even you might not make it here. Clearly, you have a lot of strength!"

"It must be from all the work I do at the theater!" Rani laughed. "Moving scenery and lugging props around takes muscles, believe me."

"I daresay it does," the Tree Queen replied, her eyes twinkling once more. "But it's not just your body's strength that got you here, Enchanted Dragon. It's also the strength of your mind. Which is lucky, because you'll need to be tough if you are to complete the quest."

Rani leaned forward, excitement fizzing through her. "What is the quest?"

The Tree Queen paused. When she spoke

again, there was regret in her voice. "I have a sister. Nowadays, she is known as the Shadow Queen. We were very close, until she became ruler of the forest. The power went to her head. She was a terrible, cruel leader! It took a long time, but we defeated her and I became the leader of the Magic Forest instead. She has been jealous of my power ever since."

Rani thought about when Anjali started acting. At first, Rani had been jealous. And even now she sometimes felt a twinge of envy, especially when Anjali got lots of praise for a performance. But mostly, Rani just felt proud. Also, she liked working backstage. Acting just wasn't Rani's thing—thank goodness! It would have been harder if she'd wanted to be an actor like her sister.

The Tree Queen continued. "My Glitter and

Treasure Dragons helped bring the Shadow Queen under control. But now she has found a way to steal the magic from the Sky Swirls. And she has created extra helpers to do her bidding."

"We saw something weird on the way here," Rani remembered. "The Questies called it a Bright Shadow."

"One of her helpers." The Tree Queen nodded. "Be wary around them! They are dangerous. The Shadow Queen used them to kidnap the trained Quest Friends."

"But why would she do that?" Rani wondered. She couldn't imagine anyone wanting to hurt the Questies.

"The Dragon Girls always have Quest Friends to guide and protect them on their adventures," the Tree Queen said. "My sister could not beat the Dragon Girls, so now she's trying to make things harder by taking away your helpers. That's not the only problem. Without fully trained Friends, the junior Questies cannot learn the skills they need. This means that now, any Dragon Girls who come to the forest won't have a helper—or the protection their Friend's love gives them."

"Is my quest to find the missing Questies?" Rani guessed.

"That's an important part of it," the queen agreed. "The other part is to rein in the Shadow Queen's power."

Rani gulped. This seemed like a lot to do. Especially on her own!

The Tree Queen reached a long branch-arm toward Rani. A chain was dangling on it, attached to a shiny tube. "Look through the

end of this," the Tree Queen instructed as Rani took the object in her claws.

Rani saw all the colors of the glade turn into an abstract pattern. She twisted the tube and the pattern changed. "It's a kaleidoscope!"

"We call it the guider-scope." The Tree Queen smiled. "Whenever you need guidance or directions, give it a twist and look through it. Your enchanted powers will give it infinite settings."

Rani slipped the chain with the guider-scope around her neck. She didn't really understand what it did or how it would help her. *But I'll figure it out when I need to,* she thought.

When she looked up, Rani saw that the queen was starting to turn back into a tree. Her gown was again becoming moss and her flowing hair was turning back into leaves.

Clearly, Rani's time with the queen was running out. But there was something very important she still needed to ask. "Where should I begin? I mean, how do I get started?"

"Head to the Quest Friends' training village," the queen replied. Rani could hardly hear her beneath the sound of rustling leaves. "I believe they call it 'Camp Questie.' I sense that there may be one left there who can assist you."

Then, with a final sway, the Tree Queen disappeared entirely into tree form.

Rani stayed on the soft grass for a moment. She knew that when she left the safety of the glade, her quest would begin. It would be exciting, but it might also be dangerous. She couldn't help wishing that she had someone to help her like all the other Dragon Girls did.

But I can do it, she reminded herself. *I HAVE to. The Tree Queen is counting on me.* In fact, the whole Magic Forest was counting on her.

Flapping her wings, Rani rose into the air and back through the shimmering force field ... and crashed straight into three excited little creatures!

"Hello! How come you're still here?" Rani exclaimed. "Didn't we say *goodbye* just before?"

"We said *goodbye for now*," Flittercub reminded Rani. "And now we're saying *hello again!*"

"I told you I was sure we'd meet again," Splishi pointed out. "And I was right."

Rani laughed. She couldn't argue with these Questies. And she was thrilled to see their sweet little faces.

"We're guessing that the Tree Queen gave you a quest," TrustyPup said.

"So . . . we're going to come with you," Splishi said.

"We know we're not real Questies. Yet," Flittercub said.

"But we want to help you anyway," TrustyPup

continued. "We're good at figuring things out . . .
at least, we are for junior Questies."

Three little faces looked hopefully at Rani.

She beamed at them. "I would love that. Do
you happen to know the way to Camp Questie
from here?"

"Of course we do!" Flittercub exclaimed.

"Almost all of the way!" TrustyPup added, wagging her tail.

"We'll probably only get a teensy bit lost!" Splishi promised.

The Sky Swirls danced across the darkening sky as Rani followed the Questies through the forest. The colors were very beautiful, but Rani was pretty sure they were more faded than before.

Is that because the Shadow Queen is stealing more of their power? she wondered, thinking back to what the Tree Queen had said.

It was a worry. But right now, Rani had to focus on keeping track of the Questies! The three little creatures would dart one way, and then another. It was obvious they weren't quite sure which way to go, but Rani pretended not to notice.

Besides, it was wonderful to explore more of the Magic Forest. They flew over a wide emerald-green river, and later past a waterfall surrounded by a shimmering mist. They saw a volcano and lush rolling fields. Farther on, they flew over what Rani at first thought was a lake of pink water. But when she swooped lower, she realized that the pink stuff was actually salt! Flying high again, Rani spotted snowcapped mountains off on the horizon. And to the south she glimpsed a glittering sea.

The more Rani saw, the more she wanted to protect this special place.

Suddenly, the three Questies stopped flying and high-fived in midair. "We did it!"

Flittercub turned to Rani. "Camp Questie is down there!" She pointed with her tail.

Rani saw what looked like an adventure playground, but up high. There were cute wooden huts set within the generous branches of the ancient trees. In the center were climbing frames and swings. There were rope bridges strung between trees. Down on the ground, Rani saw countless ponds filled with water lilies, and huge sandboxes everywhere. There was even a kind of trampoline on stilts, made of reeds and bamboo.

It looked like a very fun place to learn how to be a Questie!

As Rani and the others flew lower, she saw little creatures—junior Questies—everywhere.

They were splashing in the ponds and swinging on the ropes. Others were flying about wildly, doing somersaults in the air. Some were jumping on the trampoline, squealing with delight and flinging themselves off, landing—about half the time—in the sandboxes. It was chaos.

"Things have been a bit out of control since the trained Questies disappeared," admitted Flittercub, catching the surprised look on Rani's face.

"The big ones made sure we went to bed on time," TrustyPup said.

"And that we ate the right food," added Splishi.

"Doing whatever we wanted was fun at first," Flittercub said. "But I wish we could go back to normal now. I'm a bit sick of honeyberry pie and staying up late."

"And we want to do our training!" Splishi said. "We'd only just started when the Bright Shadows came."

"We miss the big ones a lot." TrustyPup gave a soft howl.

To Rani's dismay, the three Questies began to cry. "Don't worry!" Rani said. She tried to cuddle them in her wings, but it turned out that flying and cuddling at the same time was difficult. "Come on, let's land."

The lower they flew, the louder the noise of the camp became. The junior Questies were all laughing and yelling. It was like Rani's schoolyard at lunchtime. Rani saw a little fluffball of a kitten with bright bat wings fluttering above the pond, while a mini starfish with a horn did cartwheels across the water. Trotting across the rope bridge was a winged elk. Rani gazed at a tiny dolphin and a little purple jellyfish flying together. The jellyfish had one tentacle wrapped around the dolphin's left flipper like they were holding hands.

Rani landed on a patch of grass, being careful to avoid squishing anyone. The Questies were tiny compared to her! For a moment, they

all stopped and stared at Rani. Then, almost immediately, they went back to playing.

Flittercub, TrustyPup, and Splishi landed next to her. "Come on. We'll take you on a tour," Flittercub offered.

Together, the little group began to make their way around the village.

"Camp Questie is where we learn our skills," TrustyPup explained.

"Only the most talented animals get selected

to come here," Splishi added proudly. "Often Questies come from the same family, but not always. You must be good at finding your way around the forest, and able to stay calm in a crisis. And a Questie must be able to appear by a Dragon Girl's side the moment they sense danger."

"Questies form very strong bonds with Dragon Girls," Flittercub said, trotting by Rani's side.

"The best Questies know what a Dragon Girl is thinking almost before she's even thought it," TrustyPup said. "My brother PlushyPup was really good at sniffing out danger," she added, her tail suddenly drooping. "I miss him so much."

"We'll rescue your brother," Rani said, hating

to see the puppy looking so sad. "And all the others."

The three junior Questies cheered up immediately. "We knew you'd help," said Flittercub, nuzzling against her leg.

"How will you do it?" Splishi asked.

Rani wasn't sure what to say. The problem was, she had no idea! The Tree Queen had told her that someone in the village would be able to help her. Rani looked around. The Questies were adorable, but most of them were overtired or upside down or both. She did not think that any of them could offer much help.

Then she remembered the guider-scope that the Tree Queen had given her. She definitely needed guidance right now.

Rani lifted it up and looked through. The

object gently pulled her gaze down and to the left. At first, Rani could only see bits of color. But when she gave the guider-scope a turn, something came into view.

At the base of a tree, half-hidden by long grass, was the entrance to a tunnel. Huddled there was a mouselike creature with a pom-pom tail. It looked bigger than all the other Questies Rani had met.

He seemed to sense Rani's gaze, and turned

so that his catlike face was looking directly at her. He mouthed the words, "Help me, Dragon Girl!"

Rani let the object fall back on its chain and dashed over to the tree she'd seen through the guider-scope.

"Where are you going?" squealed the Questies, racing after her.

Rani skidded to a stop. Pushing back the long grass, she saw a tunnel. It was too small for Rani to fit inside, but she could just make out the Questie she'd seen through the guider-scope.

"Who are you?" Rani whispered.

"I'm Squeaklet," the animal replied. Even though the Questie was clearly worried, his voice was calming to Rani. "I'm the only fully trained Questie left. The Bright Shadows are searching for me. I can sense them drawing closer. But I was determined to hide until I could speak to you, Enchanted Dragon."

"I'll keep you safe," Rani promised.

"I don't know where the other Questies have been taken," Squeaklet said urgently, "but a strange thought keeps going around and around in my mind: *Sometimes goodness can be overshadowed by badness.* I am sure it's the key to finding the missing ones."

Rani frowned. Goodness can be overshadowed by badness? What did that mean?

Before she could ask anything, Rani felt a strange sensation. It was both horribly cold and burning hot at the same time.

A bright shape slithered over her shoulder. It was followed by another. And another. And another. Bright Shadows!

6

"Get away from him!" Rani roared. A golden fog filled the tiny tunnel. Was that from her roar? Rani wasn't sure and she couldn't stop to find out.

The Bright Shadows moved over Rani toward Squeaklet, making her scales itch. Worse, the Bright Shadows were wrapping themselves around Squeaklet!

Rani snapped at the shadows, trying to reach deeper into the tunnel so she could rescue Squeaklet. But she was too big and the

shadows were too quick. They surrounded the little creature.

With a flash of blinding light, the shadows pushed past Rani and out into the air.

Rani wriggled back out of the tight space. "They've got Squeaklet!" Rani told the junior Questies.

"That way!" Flittercub cried, pointing at a glowing streak in the sky.

Rani launched herself into the air after them. "I've got to get him back." She'd promised Squeaklet she would keep him safe. Now he had been taken, right before her eyes. She *had* to save him.

"We're coming!" TrustyPup barked, and the three Questies leapt into the sky behind her.

"No, you stay here and be safe," Rani called over her shoulder. "I'll be fine!"

The last thing Rani wanted was any more creatures being stolen by those terrible Bright Shadows.

Camp Questie was soon far behind as Rani chased after Squeaklet and the Bright Shadows. The shadows zoomed across the sky like a comet as other Bright Shadows emerged from the dark forest to join them.

The Sky Swirls, on the other hand, were definitely getting dimmer. Rani clenched her jaw. This had to be the Shadow Queen's work. How much time was left before the queen drained the swirls of their power completely? Rani had no idea. But she knew she had to stop the Shadow Queen before it was too late.

Rani surged forward. She felt strong and full of energy. But every time she got close to the glowing mass, a cluster of Bright Shadows would break from the pack and dart at her. They forced Rani back with their dazzling light and strange cold-hot energy. Over and over Rani nearly caught up, only to be pushed back.

Rani noticed something strange, though. It was only ever the shadows at the front of the pack that attacked her. Those at the back of the group never came near her. Their glow was softer and warmer, too.

Are they older, perhaps? Or are they the younger ones? Rani wasn't sure. But there was definitely something different about them.

The shadow cluster continued to fly higher and higher. They darted through a large white cloud. Rani let out a cry as the cloud turned to dust.

A moment later, the Bright Shadows swooped low, skimming across the treetops. Any leaves they touched instantly changed into wriggling lizards, which scampered down the tree trunks, leaving the trees bare of leaves.

When the shadows streaked past an apple tree, the fruit transformed into red spiders that scurried off in all directions.

Rani roared with dismay.

If the Bright Shadows were affecting clouds and leaves and fruit like this, what was happening to poor Squeaklet deep inside that swirling, glowing mass?

"Let Squeaklet go!" Rani roared, a golden mist billowing out of her again.

But it was clear the Bright Shadows had no intention of stopping. Some of the biggest, shiniest ones whirled around Rani, hissing into her face and wrapping themselves around her wings.

Rani felt the sting of their touch again, but luckily they didn't seem to affect her in any other way. *Is it because I'm the Enchanted Dragon?* she wondered.

Whatever the reason, Rani was very glad her wings hadn't turned to dust ... or spiders!

The Bright Shadows were now down in the trees, creating hundreds of leaf-lizards in their wake. Rani followed close behind. "You can't get away from me!" Rani roared.

Once again, a golden, twinkling cloud appeared, and this time Rani was sure it had come from her. The gold cloud of her roar whooshed out and engulfed a leaf-lizard. It instantly turned back to a leaf!

Rani felt a jolt of surprise. Quickly, she roared again, this time over a cluster of red spiders clinging to a branch. As the fog of her roar covered them, the spiders turned back into juicy, shiny apples.

That's so cool! Rani marveled. *My roar can undo the Bright Shadows' toxic magic.*

The Tree Queen had told Rani she would

discover she had all kinds of powers. This one was definitely going to come in handy.

Just then, the mass of Bright Shadows separated and fanned themselves out across the sky like a wall of light. Rani tried to stop, but she was going far too fast! She flew right through the Bright Shadows. Her ears hummed with a high-pitched sound, and her eyes were so dazzled that for a moment she couldn't see anything.

At full speed, Rani slammed into a tree and the air was pushed from her lungs. Rani tumbled to the ground, crashing through the branches as she fell, hard. For a moment Rani lay frozen, unable to cry out or move. Finally, she drew in a gasping breath and cautiously opened one eye, then the other.

She had landed in some kind of gloomy swamp. Above her hovered a cold mist, making it hard to see more than a few feet away.

Looking up, Rani could just make out the Sky Swirls. But there was no sign of the Bright Shadows . . . or of any other living creature, for that matter.

Rani suddenly felt very alone. "Hello?" she

roared. "Anyone there?" In the swampy darkness, her roar seemed warm and comforting. It reminded Rani of when she rubbed a patch clear on the bathroom mirror after she'd taken a shower. But soon the golden light faded.

Suddenly, Rani's ears began to hum just like when she'd slammed into the wall of Bright Shadows. *There's danger here!* she thought, tensing.

A figure stepped out from behind a huge moss-covered rock, so bright that Rani had to shield her eyes. But she could guess who this was. The thumping of her heart had already told her.

"Well, Enchanted Dragon," the Shadow Queen said. Her voice made Rani's face feel hot and caused a shiver to run down her spine at the same time. "What a *pleasure* it is to meet you."

Rani frowned at the Shadow Queen. "What have you done with Squeaklet?" she demanded. "And all the other Questies?"

The Shadow Queen gave a nasty, glimmering smile. "Don't worry yourself about that, Dragon Girl. All those weird little animals are fine. They are closer than you realize, in fact."

Rani looked around the swamp. Were the

Questies hidden somewhere nearby? But the glare from the Shadow Queen combined with the thick fog made it impossible to see very far. All Rani could be sure about were the Bright Shadows, whirling about their queen in the gloom.

She stared at the shadows. Were some of them still wrapped around Squeaklet? It didn't look like it. So where was he? Had the shadows left him in the forest somewhere? Or had some of them taken him to another place?

Now that she was looking closely, Rani noticed that each of the shadows was a different shape and size. One shadow broke away from the pack and darted toward her. Rani tensed, ready to leap out of the way or roar in defense. But before the shadow reached her, two others whooshed over and shoved it back into the group.

Rani didn't know what to make of what she'd

seen. Had those two shadows just stopped her from being attacked by the first shadow? Maybe. But Rani had a feeling that the first shadow hadn't wanted to hurt her. There was a warmth to it that the others lacked. And maybe she'd imagined it, but Rani could have sworn it had a pom-pom shadow tail.

"You can't beat me, Dragon Girl," the Shadow Queen said. "I am far too strong. And I will keep getting stronger." The queen reached her hands toward the sky. "Sky Swirls, listen to me!"

The queen began muttering softly. Rani couldn't make out all the words, but it sounded like some sort of spell. Suddenly, the queen spread out her fingers and her whisper became a shout. "Give me POWER!"

Coils of color streamed down from the Sky Swirls, flowing into each of the Shadow Queen's long fingers. She immediately glowed more brightly, while the Sky Swirls looked paler.

"You can't do that!" Rani cried, shocked.

"Clearly, I can, Dragon Girl. Sky Swirl magic is there for anyone to take," the Shadow Queen retorted. "I am just the only one who's worked out the spell to do so. Why wait for the magic to fall down and be shared when I can have it all for myself?"

"That magic is for the whole forest, not just you!" Rani felt her anger rising. She hated greediness. At home—and at school, and the theater—Rani was used to everyone sharing whatever they had.

Sometimes that might be cake. Sometimes

it might be ideas or information. Sometimes it might be sharing some extra time to help someone else.

The Shadow Queen sneered, folding her arms. "Why would I share? That would mess up my plans to take over as ruler of the Magic Forest."

The queen rose and flew in a loop, leaving a smear of painfully bright light in her wake. Then, as if testing out her strength, she brushed past some vines that were dangling from a tree. The vines turned into long green snakes, hissing, and struggling to free themselves from their branches.

"Stop that!" Rani roared.

Her gold, misty roar billowed out like a cloud, completely covering the vine-snakes. When the roar cleared, the snakes had turned back into vines.

Annoyance flashed across the queen's face. Then she gave a slow, cold smile. "Impressive, Dragon Girl," she said. "Let's see what else you can do."

Before Rani could respond, the Shadow Queen began whooshing around the swamp, followed by her Bright Shadows. She brushed past a tree, turning it to white, crumbly chalk. A mossy stone became a wriggling pile of croaking toads. She swooped down low and turned the swamp waters into an oily, sticky goop.

Rani launched herself into the air, following the queen wherever she went and roaring loudly to undo each of the queen's enchantments.

How can I stop her? Rani thought desperately. She couldn't just fly behind the Shadow Queen forever, undoing the damage. She had to find the missing Questies. If only she had some help!

Suddenly, one of the Bright Shadows again broke from the group and darted toward her. Rani recognized it! It was the same shadow with the pom-pom tail that had tried to approach her last time. Once again, others shot out to stop it. But this time the shadow dodged them and flew right by Rani's ear. It whispered something. Something familiar.

Sometimes goodness can be overshadowed by badness.

Rani whirled around to look at the shadow as it sped by. She thought she knew what was going on. But she needed to be sure. Rani lifted the guider-scope to her eye and looked through it. At first, she could only see the glare of the Bright Shadow. But with a satisfying click, she twisted the device, and now, instead of a Bright Shadow, Rani saw Squeaklet!

I knew it! Her pulse racing, Rani ran the guider-scope over the other Bright Shadows. Some of them completely disappeared when viewed through the lens. But others turned into a variety of cute little creatures. Questies! Rani spotted a flying mini dolphin, and a bird with multicolored wings and a unicorn horn. There was also a flying lion cub who looked exactly like Flittercub, only bigger.

Rani let go of the guider-scope and confronted the Shadow Queen. "You turned the Questies into Bright Shadows!"

She felt a whoosh of icy-cold and burning-hot air as the Shadow Queen loomed in front of her. Her glowing eyes were fixed on Rani. "Well done, Enchanted Dragon," she said, not sounding remotely pleased. "You worked it out. You are more talented than I thought. But this knowledge is of no use. Your little roar will never be powerful enough to reverse the spell I've placed upon those creatures."

The Shadow Queen was so close, Rani had

to fight the urge to back away. "Why are you doing this?" she asked.

"It's all the Tree Queen's fault!" The Shadow Queen frowned. "She left me with no choice. Did she tell you that we are sisters?"

Rani nodded. "She said you were jealous when she became the leader of the Magic Forest."

"I wasn't jealous," the Shadow Queen hissed. "I just knew I'd make a better ruler. She can't even do magic!"

"That's not true," Rani said. "I've seen her change from a tree into a person. You need a lot of magic to do that."

The Shadow Queen gave a scornful laugh. "She can only partly transform herself. She is stuck in the ground and cannot leave her glade. Can you guess who put that spell on her?"

Rani stared at the Shadow Queen in shock. "You turned your own sister into a tree?"

Sometimes Rani and Anjali argued. All siblings argue. But this was a different level altogether.

The Shadow Queen's eyes blazed. "She should have let me stay ruler. And until I am queen once more, the Tree Queen will be stuck there. No one will get in my way."

Once again, the Shadow Queen began to whirl through the air, her fingers outstretched. Rani heard her muttering the same quiet spell as she pulled in more Sky Swirl magic.

She hovered above Rani, shining with power. When she spoke, her voice seemed to fill the forest. "So tell me, Enchanted Dragon. Will you join my side by choice, or must I turn you into a Bright Shadow? Either way, I win."

The Bright Shadows whipped around and around Rani, so dazzling that she had to look away. Rani now knew that many of these shadows were actually enchanted Questies. But while they were under the Shadow Queen's spell, she needed to be extremely careful around them.

Every part of Rani's dragon body tensed as she desperately tried to figure out what to do next.

Then another sound pierced the air. It was three little voices, calling to her in unison. "Roar, Enchanted Dragon! ROAR!"

As Flittercub, TrustyPup, and Splishi flew closer, Rani breathed in deeply, filling her lungs. She held her breath for a moment, thinking about the impossible choice the Shadow Queen had presented to her: join the Shadow Queen or become a shadow herself.

Rani chose neither!

The Shadow Queen had said Rani's roar

wasn't powerful enough to undo the enchantment on the Questies. But Rani wanted to test it out for herself. The roar she released was bigger, more golden, and more twinkly than any of her previous roars. The magical mist spread across the entire swamp.

"What are you doing?" the Shadow Queen snarled. "Stop that at once!" She surged into the air, and the Bright Shadows followed as if connected by invisible string.

But Rani had no intention of stopping. When she ran out of air, she refilled her lungs and roared again.

"You're roaring the swamp away!" Flittercub cried as TrustyPup and Splishi cartwheeled in delight.

The twinkling glow of Rani's roar was melting the swampy gloom! In its place, a beautiful meadow appeared, with tall, graceful trees and sleeping flowers. A little stream flowed over smooth stones. It was all gently lit by the Sky Swirls floating above. Squeaklet's words came back to her. The goodness of this place had been overshadowed by badness!

The Shadow Queen flew back and forth, her fury making her shine brighter. "You'll regret this, Dragon Girl! One word from me and my Bright Shadows will attack you and your foolish little friends."

It was true that some of the Bright Shadows looked ready to fight. But others—the ones with the softer glow—looked like they were trying to pull away from their queen. Rani was positive the enchanted Questies would not want to attack. But would they be able to resist the Shadow Queen's bright power?

I can't do spells like the Shadow Queen, but my roar lifted the swamp's enchantment, Rani thought. *Maybe I CAN undo the spell on the Questies?*

Flittercub, TrustyPup, and Splishi hovered nearby. "We believe in you!" TrustyPup said.

So once again, Rani filled her chest with air. She flew as close as she dared to the glowing shadows before releasing her powerful roar.

But nothing happened! The shadows all stayed exactly how they were.

"Nice try!" The Shadow Queen laughed. "It's cute how you Dragon Girls always think your pathetic roars will fix everything. But I told you it wouldn't work. My spells cannot be undone by huffing and puffing." She tilted her head to the side thoughtfully. "Perhaps you'd like to find that out for yourself?"

Before Rani realized what was happening, the three little Questies shoved her to one side with surprising force. They were only just in time, for a moment later, a streak of blinding light flashed past.

"She tried to turn you into a Bright Shadow!"

Splishi cried, wide-eyed with outrage.

"We won't let her!" Flittercub said.

"No way!" TrustyPup agreed. "She'll have to turn us into Bright Shadows first."

The junior Questies glared at the Shadow Queen as she raised her hands, preparing to send another glowing streak at Rani. Splishi, Flittercub, and TrustyPup zoomed in front of Rani to protect her.

Rani felt her heart filling. These three tiny creatures were so brave! But how would they fare against the Shadow Queen's immense power? Rani didn't want to risk finding out.

She was on high alert now, ready to scoop up the Questies and dash to safety. She was just as determined to protect these little creatures as they were to protect her.

Suddenly, words spilled out of her from somewhere deep inside:

With my wings and with my roar
I'll keep them safe forevermore.

Shimmering air appeared between the Questies and the Shadow Queen. It looked like the force field around the Tree Queen's glade!

"What's going on?" Rani asked, looking at the others.

"You just cast a spell!" Splishi squeaked.

Rani stared, confused. "I did?"

TrustyPup nodded. "That's a protection spell. They're the most powerful."

Rani felt a shiver of excitement. She'd always wanted to be able to do spells!

The Shadow Queen flew at them, but she couldn't get past the shield. A strange look flashed across her angry face. "That spell won't last. And you've given me an interesting idea. When I turned the Questies into Bright Shadows, I didn't bother transforming the juniors. I assumed they were useless and cowardly. But I see I was wrong."

Rani watched the Shadow Queen, dread growing inside her.

"There are two things you might not know about me," the Shadow Queen continued. "Firstly, I am prepared to admit when I've made a mistake. And secondly, when I make a mistake, I correct it."

The queen whooshed into the air and, with a harsh flash of light, disappeared between the trees, her Bright Shadows streaking behind her.

"Where is she going?" Rani wondered aloud. But as the words left her mouth, she realized she knew the answer. And from the look on their faces, so did the Questies. *The Shadow Queen is heading to Camp Questie to bewitch the juniors!*

"We have to get there first!" Rani said urgently.

Instantly, she felt the guider-scope tug on its chain around her neck. Rani lifted it to her eye and gave the device a twist in the opposite direction from last time. A tunnel appeared, glowing with an eerie purple light. Through the tunnel, Rani could see Camp Questie! But was it really there? If she flew through it, would she actually get to the village, or would she simply crash into another tree?

There's only one way to find out, Rani decided.

"Questies, climb onto my back," she called. "And hold on tight."

With the Questies on board, Rani sped into the tunnel.

The tunnel was a magical shortcut! As Rani flew into it, it closed up behind her. Ahead, the village grew steadily bigger. Flittercub, TrustyPup, and Splishi held on, squealing with joy as they hurtled along.

The tunnel ended suddenly, and Rani shot out. She somersaulted once and landed right in the middle of the compound. The last time Rani had been here, the village was swarming with very loud junior Questies.

Now the village was silent.

"Where is everyone?" Rani muttered, looking around. *Were they too late? Surely the Shadow Queen hadn't beaten them?* Then she heard a strange rumbling.

"Snoring!" Flittercub giggled.

TrustyPup nodded. "They've finally tired themselves out."

"Where do you all sleep?" Rani asked.

She hoped they had a head start on the Shadow Queen and her Bright Shadows. But Rani was pretty sure they'd be here soon. She had to get everyone ready before the attack!

"In the sleeping hut," Splishi said. "This way."

Splishi led the way to a group of tree huts. Each had a thatched roof and wide deck. The huts were all connected by swinging ropes and little bridges.

Splishi landed on the deck of the biggest hut and disappeared inside, followed by TrustyPup and Flittercub. Rani managed to squeeze in, too, but only just! The tiny doors were not made for dragons.

The hut was filled with rows and rows of bunk beds. On each was a sleeping figure. There were other types of beds, too. Perches for the feathery Questies jutted out from the walls. And in the middle of the hut was a big curved tank.

"That's for the juniors who sleep in water," TrustyPup explained.

Rani could just make out the tiny silver dolphin and little starfish she'd seen holding hands earlier. Their eyes were shut and their little bodies drifted gently in the water as they slept.

There was something so adorable about a hut full of tiny sleeping creatures! Rani could hardly bear to wake them.

But Flittercub, TrustyPup, and Splishi

obviously didn't mind. "WAKE UP, EVERYONE!" they called, flapping around the hut.

Most of the sleeping creatures didn't even stir. One of them groaned from the bunk bed, "No way. We only just went to sleep."

"We thought it would be fun to stay up forever," mumbled the rainbow-colored bird from a perch, head firmly tucked under a wing. "But it's not as fun as it sounds."

"Come back later." The silvery dolphin in the tank yawned, flipping its tail sleepily.

"We can't come back later. The Shadow Queen is on her way," Rani said in her loud dragon voice. "If you don't all get up now, you'll be turned into Bright Shadows."

That woke everyone up! Soon, Rani was surrounded by little Questies, all looking at her with a mixture of excitement and fear.

"The Shadow Queen is coming back here?"

"Does this mean she turned all the big Questies into Bright Shadows? That's terrible!"

"No way will we let her do that to us. We'll stop her!"

Once again, Rani marveled at the bravery of these junior Questies. They were tiny, but they had dragon-sized courage. All the same, she was not going to risk any of them getting hurt.

"The best thing you can do is hide," she explained. "The Shadow Queen is dangerous and I need to keep you all safe." Rani turned to Flittercub, TrustyPup, and Splishi. "That includes you three. I can't have you getting turned into shadows—not when I don't know how to undo the spell. I will battle the queen by myself."

Rani hoped she sounded convincing. She was willing to do anything to protect these little animals. But secretly, the idea of facing the Shadow Queen alone was daunting.

"We're not going to hide," Flittercub said firmly.

"No way," TrustyPup agreed. "For as long as there have been Dragon Girls, there have been Questies by their side. We can't let you fight that Shadow Queen on your own. It goes against the Questie Code."

Rani tried a different tack. "Am I right in thinking that Questies are honor bound to do what Dragon Girls want?" she asked slowly.

"Well, yes, they are," Splishi admitted, frowning. Then she beamed again. "But we're only junior Questies, so that rule doesn't apply to us!"

Rani half sighed, half laughed. Getting the Questies to hide was impossible. "Okay," she said. "But it's up to you three to keep the others in line. Or at least try to."

"Don't worry, we will," Flittercub promised.

"We'll do some warm-ups with them all right now," TrustyPup said.

"And when the Shadow Queen arrives, we'll be ready," Splishi added.

Flittercub, TrustyPup, and Splishi flew up near the roof of the sleeping hut.

"Listen up, everyone!" Flittercub called. "We might not have had much training, but that doesn't mean that we can't beat the Shadow Queen."

"We were all chosen to become Questies, after all," Splishi added.

"Exactly." TrustyPup nodded. "We're smart and fast and good at thinking on our feet. We just need to stay calm, keep our eyes open, and listen to one another."

A hush had fallen over the sleeping hut. Everyone was listening carefully.

"We suspect the Shadow Queen and her helpers are on their way here now," Rani said.

"But we'll be ready," Splishi said. "We'll dive from the tops of the trees! Shoot up from the ponds. We'll fly around and around so the Bright Shadows get dizzy chasing us. We don't want to hurt them, because some of them are enchanted Questies. But we do want to tire them out."

"Do you really think we can beat them?" asked the rainbow bird with the horn.

"Of course we can!" Flittercub said. "Because we're not just doing this to save ourselves."

"We're doing it to protect the Enchanted Dragon," TrustyPup finished. "And to rescue the big Questies."

Rani felt her eyes fill with tears. The bravery of these tiny Questies!

There was a shout from over near the window. "Something weird is happening to the sky," a tiny elk-like creature called. "It's all glowy."

"The Sky Swirls?" Rani asked. But her stomach had already started to churn.

The Questie shook her head. "I don't think so."

In a flash, Rani was out of the hut. The sky was indeed glowing, but this had the harsh glare of bad magic. Turning back, Rani saw all the Questies watching her from the windows of the hut.

They looked small and defenseless. But Rani knew that looks could be deceiving. "Get ready, junior Questies," she called. She was pleased that her powerful dragon voice sounded steady, betraying not a single hint of her nerves. "The Shadow Queen is here."

10

The glare grew brighter and brighter, zooming toward them like a fireball. The Shadow Queen was in the center of the glow, surrounded by her Bright Shadows.

Rani's heart pounded. There seemed to be even more shadows than before. How was one Dragon Girl—plus all these little untrained

Questies—going to fight the queen and her shadows?

Flittercub nudged her. "Don't worry about us, Enchanted Dragon." She grinned. "Just because we're cute doesn't mean we can't also be fierce!"

"And don't let the Shadow Queen scare you," TrustyPup said. "She probably uses all that glare to seem bigger than she really is. I bet that underneath it all, she's not so scary."

Rani smiled. Somehow these little Questies always said the right thing.

"Are we ready to do this?" Splishi called.

Rani nodded just as the Shadow Queen and the Bright Shadows swirled into the village. As they darted around, some of the bridges between the huts caught on fire. And so did one of the huts! The Shadow Queen whooshed by the rope ladders, turning them into hissing pythons, twisting around one another.

"Don't waste your time trying to fight me," the Shadow Queen cried in her hot-cold voice. "Just give up now."

The young voices of the Questies sang out: "Give up? No way!"

The air filled with the sound of tiny wings, beating furiously. The junior Questies darted at the queen from every direction. They dove down from up high, then whirled around her. Others flew in from the side, scooping up sand from the sandbox and flinging it into the air, dulling the glare. Other Questies surged into the ponds, flicking up arcs of water with their wings or tails to put out the fires. They also

drenched the Bright Shadows as they passed, slowing them down.

Taking in a gulp of air, Rani added a huge misty roar to the mayhem. It whirled around the village like a cloud, turning the pythons back into rope ladders. Rani flew back and forth, urging the Questies on. "Keep on moving! You're doing great!"

If the queen and her shadows couldn't catch the Questies, then they couldn't turn them into Bright Shadows. Then Rani had another thought: What if she could separate the enchanted Questies from the ordinary Bright Shadows? With their softer glow and Questie-ish shapes, Rani was pretty sure she could pick them out.

Even as she thought this, Flittercub, TrustyPup, and Splishi appeared, out of breath but focused. Rani explained her plan and they all nodded. "Great idea!" Flittercub said. "We'll do our best to round them up somehow!"

The Shadow Queen's furious shouting cut through the confusion. "Do you truly think you can outsmart me? You have forgotten that I have access to extra power."

She raised her arms, stretched out her claw-like fingers, and began to chant:

Swirling power in the air
Come and feed my shadow's glare
You're all mine—and not to share
I'll take it all, with none to spare!

Rani watched even more color draining from the sky. "If you don't stop, I'll—"

The Shadow Queen cut her off, laughing. "You'll what? Attack me? I'd like to see you try." She lunged at Rani. Her newly charged glare was impossibly bright in the darkness. "You and these puny, half-baked critters will never win against me."

She flicked her long fingers and a stream

of white-hot light shot out, striking a nearby Questie. The little creature gave a cry and, to Rani's horror, turned into a Bright Shadow.

Rani roared. "Don't you dare!" Her roar engulfed the newly transformed Bright Shadow. For a brief moment, it turned back into a Questie, but then became a Bright Shadow once more.

"See?" the Shadow Queen taunted. "You're simply not strong enough. But don't feel bad, Dragon Girl. I have been planning this for a long time. I would never let a Dragon Girl and a few babies stop me."

"Taking the Sky Swirl power for yourself is wrong and unfair," Rani said, her voice shaking.

"Unfair?" the Shadow Queen sneered. "I'll tell you what's unfair: my sister taking over as ruler of the Magic Forest! It's obvious I was the better leader. The Sky Swirls are simply helping me get back what I deserve. Now, get out of my way. I have junior Questies to catch."

The Shadow Queen pushed past her, in pursuit of another junior.

Rani was about to give chase when a thought stopped her. What if *she* used some Sky Swirl power, like the Shadow Queen? Would it make her strong enough to break the spell on the enchanted Questies?

Doubts flooded her. She knew that the Sky Swirls were very powerful. What if Rani wasn't strong enough—or magical enough—to tap into that power? *And even if I can do it, it's wrong*, she reminded herself. *If the Shadow Queen shouldn't do it, then neither should I.*

Splishi swooped into view, the others close behind. "I know you're worried about doing what the Shadow Queen has done. But you don't want the power for selfish reasons. You'd use it to help us."

"If you can do it, topping up your power with Sky Swirl magic is a good idea," TrustyPup said, an anxious look in her big eyes. "The juniors are putting up a brave fight, but the queen and her shadows are winning."

Rani looked up to see two more Questies transformed into Bright Shadows. Behind them, another group of Questies was trying to separate the enchanted shadows from the rest of the pack. The problem was that the moment they did, the Bright Shadows would swish over and pull them back again.

"Please try it, Enchanted Dragon," Flittercub

urged. "We need help. Plus, if you take some magic, there's less for the Shadow Queen to steal."

Rani knew the Questies were right. It was vital that she got that extra burst of magic. She just hoped she could pull it off! Maybe she could try a spell to stop the Shadow Queen from seeing what she was doing? As before, Rani felt the words forming inside her as if they'd always been there:

Hide me from the shadow's eyes
While I draw power from the skies

She felt a mist wrap around her and knew that it would shield her from the Shadow Queen's view. For how long, she wasn't sure! She quickly flew upward. As she got closer to the Sky Swirls, Rani felt their energy like a warm breeze against her scales. How could she harness their magic? She felt a rumble in her chest, the feeling she now knew was another spell brewing.

Sky Swirls, Sky Swirls, listen well
I need your help to break this spell
And then I will return the power
To every creature, tree, and flower!

She breathed in and a swirly warmth flowed into her. It was like a roar, but in reverse. Rani breathed in deeper this time, drawing in more swirls. She tingled as the energy seeped into her. How much magic could she breathe in? There was only one way to find out.

Rani darted through the swirls, gulping at them. Was she imagining it, or did the pink ones taste a little like strawberry and the green ones like lime? Either way, the more Sky Swirls she breathed in, the stronger she felt.

Suddenly, there was a loud cry of rage from below. "Nooo! Where are all the Sky Swirls going?"

Rani didn't bother replying. She breathed in the last few stray swirls, and flew back down. As she approached the village, she sensed that the junior Questies were growing tired, although they showed no signs of giving up.

A mix of feelings tumbled in Rani. Fury at the Shadow Queen, pride in the Questies, and a little bit of fear. What if she still wasn't powerful enough to beat the queen? But she would not let the doubts get to her.

Rani roared, the Sky Swirls magic pouring out. She watched as it spun and looped through the air, the colors even brighter now than when they'd been in the sky. *My roar is giving the swirls extra strength!*

It was nice to think that Rani was giving something back, rather than just taking something from the forest.

"Attack her!" the Shadow Queen commanded her shadows, her long hair whipping around her face.

A mass of Bright Shadow surged into the swirling, twinkling billow of Rani's roar.

Rani held her breath as they collided.

There was a high, tinkling sound, like glass smashing. Many of the Bright Shadows vanished into puffs of twinkling dust. But one shadow quivered for a moment, then, with a loud pop, turned back into a very dazed-looking, winged lion cub.

11

Flittercub gave a shout of delight. "Buttercub!" The little lion cub flew over and threw her paws around the bigger one. "I'm so happy to see you," she purred.

But someone else was not happy.

"How dare you try to ruin my plans!" the Shadow Queen howled. "I command you to stop immediately!" She whooshed at Rani, who easily dodged out of the way.

Rani felt faster than ever. Faster, and more powerful. She breathed in deeply, ready to roar again. But before she could, TrustyPup flew over to one of the Bright Shadows. "PlushyPup!" he cried. "I'd know you anywhere!"

"No, TrustyPup!" Rani called. "They're still enchanted. You might get hurt!"

But it was too late. The little puppy reached out and touched the Bright Shadow with her nose. Once again, the sound of shattering glass filled the air . . . and with a pop, another puppy appeared! He looked exactly like TrustyPup, only bigger. His tail was waggling just as furiously.

"You broke the spell!" he barked excitedly at his little sister. "I'm so proud of you."

"Actually, it was the Dragon Girl who did most of the work," TrustyPup said. "But we helped."

With a little cry, Splishi also flapped over to a shadow. "I'm sure that's my cousin Splashi!"

The moment her flippers made contact with the shadow, the spell was broken. Splishi wrapped her flippers around the pink penguin with big blue eyes who had appeared.

"You'll regret this!" the Shadow Queen thundered. She raised her hands, shooting bright ribbons of light through the air.

But the junior Questies barely noticed. One by one they spotted the shapes of their siblings, cousins, friends, and mentors among the Bright Shadows. Each time a junior Questie touched the older one, the enchantment shattered.

The air was filled with the sounds of joy. Everywhere Rani looked she saw happy Questies, hugging and laughing. She felt like she might explode!

The Shadow Queen also looked like she

might explode—but not from joy. She shot into the air, her rage so bright that she lit up the sky.

Silence fell across the village.

"I don't need those enchanted Questies," the queen declared. "They never worked very hard for me anyway. Ordinary shadows are far easier to bend to my will." She pointed at the shadow her light was casting on a nearby tree. A bolt of burning light shot from her finger and hit the tree's shadow. It began to curl off the ground, glowing brighter and brighter as it drifted toward the Shadow Queen.

"See?" the queen said triumphantly, peeling up the shadows of the surrounding rocks, bushes, and trees. "My powers are endless. I can rebuild a shadow army in no time."

Rani didn't reply. Dawn was just beginning to break and the warmth of the new day was mixing with the aroma of strawberries and lime. *I smell Sky Swirl magic!* Rani realized. She could feel more magic seeping into her.

"The Shadow Queen's spell was strong," Buttercub said, "but yours is stronger. The Sky Swirls are drawn to you."

"Sky Swirls are always more powerful when shared," said PlushyPup wisely.

"It's time for you to give up," Rani called to the Shadow Queen.

The queen's glow was rapidly fading. "Don't tell me what to do!" she screeched, furiously zapping shadow after shadow. "You're just like my sister, always thinking you know best. When I rule this forest once more, everyone will do what I say." The queen flicked her hand at some newly formed Bright Shadows and they whooshed over to Rani.

In one move, Rani sliced at the shadows with her tail, and they fluttered back down to where they had come from.

"Go, Dragon Girl!" whooped the Questies, doing midair somersaults.

The Shadow Queen was starting to look like an ordinary shadow. Her glow was almost entirely gone. Rani, on the other hand, felt brighter and stronger than ever. She knew that she could easily overpower the queen now.

One quick roar would probably make her vanish. But somehow, that didn't feel right. "You have no helpers left," Rani pointed out after she had turned the remaining Bright Shadows back into normal shadows. "Admit it, it's over. Let's go and talk with your sister."

"I don't need helpers," the Shadow Queen yelled, but her voice sounded weak. "And I will

NEVER give up!" With a toss of her head, she turned and fled across the dawn sky.

Rani took off after her, soaking in the remaining swirls as they streamed from the Shadow Queen. Rani couldn't let the Shadow Queen out of her sight. But it was hard to see her now that her evil glow was gone. Rani needed her sharp dragon hearing to follow her through the forest.

She stopped flying, scanning the forest around her. Where had the queen gone? Had she lost her? Rani's heart sank. How terrible it would be to fail when she was so close to completing the quest.

She felt a tug at her neck. The guider-scope! Rani held the object to her eye and gave it a twist.

Nothing.

Unless... what was that huddled against that tree trunk? Rani gave the guider-scope another half twist and a girl came into focus. She had long dark hair draped across her face.

Her eyes were closed and her chest heaved. She looked so exhausted that Rani's heart filled with pity.

Rani let the guider-scope fall on its chain. The Shadow Queen was where the tired child had been. Carefully, Rani padded closer. All her fear of the queen had vanished.

"She never supported me," the Shadow Queen was muttering, her eyes still shut. "All I wanted was her approval. But she was always so critical of me! She never liked anything I did! And then she stole the leadership from me."

"Your sister?" asked Rani, her voice soft.

The Shadow Queen nodded.

"I guess that's the problem with being the ruler of the Magic Forest," Rani said thoughtfully. "It's a huge job and not everyone will like what you do. You have to be really selfless to do it well."

Slowly, the Shadow Queen opened her eyes and looked at Rani. It was clear she'd never thought about that. "Everyone thinks she's so much better than I am," she grumbled.

"I have a sister, too," Rani said. "She's amazing. *Really* amazing. It's hard being compared to her. I sometimes feel like I'll never be as great as she is."

The Shadow Queen didn't say anything, but Rani could tell she was listening.

"Anjali is leaving home soon," Rani continued. "I'm scared that she'll forget about me. Maybe she'll even be glad to get away from her annoying little sister. But do you know what I keep telling myself?"

The Shadow Queen waited for her to continue.

"I keep telling myself that she loves me," Rani finished.

The Shadow Queen's expression fell. "Then that's the difference between us, Dragon Girl. My sister doesn't feel that way about me." Her voice was gruff, but Rani heard sadness in it.

Rani tilted her head. "I'm not so sure. How about we go to her glade and ask?"

The Shadow Queen hesitated. She looked doubtful and hopeful all at once.

Just then, Rani heard a noise behind her. An excited bundle of Questies flew into view. They surrounded Rani, hugging her with their tiny paws and flapping flippers.

"You caught the Shadow Queen!" Splishi cried.

"I didn't really catch her," Rani said. "I just found her. I think she needs our help, actually."

"Help with what?" asked Flittercub.

"With talking to the Tree Queen," said Rani. "It's time for them to figure things out."

TrustyPup gave a sudden yelp. "She's gone!"

Rani looked over to where the Shadow Queen had been only a moment ago. She had indeed vanished.

"Look, she left something," Splishi said.

There, on the ground, was a closed flower. As Rani touched it with her paw, the petals opened and a tendril of smoke twisted through the air, writing floating words.

I can't speak with my sister yet.

You don't need to worry, though.

I don't want to be the ruler of the

Magic Forest again.

Tell her I'm sorry, and give her this.

The floating words faded.

It's like Squeaklet said, Rani thought. *The Shadow Queen's goodness got overshadowed by badness. But her goodness is still in there.*

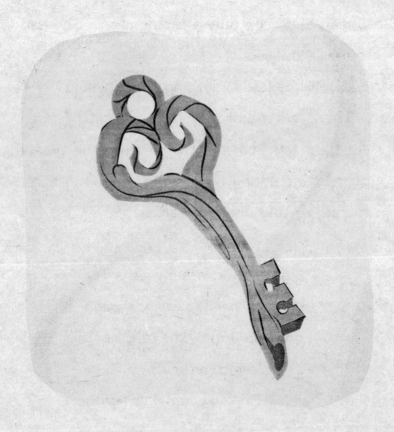

"What did she leave for the Tree Queen?" Flittercub asked, looking around.

"Maybe that flower bud?" TrustyPup suggested.

Rani picked up the flower, and saw something hidden below. It looked like a key of some kind, formed from a twisted tree root.

"What is it?" Splishi asked.

"No idea," Rani said. "But I have a feeling the Tree Queen will know."

The three junior Questies rose into the air, fluttering excitedly. "Is it time for you to return to the glade?"

Rani nodded, laughing at their endless energy. "But on the way, I have one final important task."

"What's the task?" Splishi asked.

"I still have lots of Sky Swirl magic inside me," Rani reminded her. "Normally, it floats down from the sky and gives the whole forest a magical boost, right? Well, I want to try roaring that magic out of me."

"That's a great idea!" Flittercub said.

"I am not sure if it will work," Rani admitted. "But it's worth a try."

"We'll come," TrustyPup barked.

Rani was touched. "Don't you want to spend time with your brothers and sisters and cousins, now that the Shadow Queen's spell has been lifted?"

Every single Questie shook their heads.

"A Questie always helps their Dragon Girl to the end of the adventure," PlushyPup explained solemnly.

"It's part of the Questie Code," Buttercub added.

"We're proud of these little ones," Splashi said. "They've formed very strong bonds with you. That usually only happens with fully trained Questies."

Rani beamed. She, too, was proud of her little friends. "These three are going to make great Questies," she told the older creatures. "I couldn't have done this without them."

With a flap of her wings, Rani rose into the air with the little ones, who zoomed in front to lead the way.

The other Questies waved furiously. "Come and visit Camp Questie any time you like!" they called. "You're always welcome, Enchanted Dragon."

"Thank you! Goodbye!" Rani called back.

The pink-orange glow of dawn lit up Rani's shiny scales as she surged above the treetops. The Magic Forest stretched out below her. It was, without a doubt, the most beautiful place she'd ever seen.

A rumbling feeling grew in Rani's chest until a roar burst from her. Like last time, her roar was alive with curling, twisting coils of color. The Sky Swirls fizzed with bright energy. Rani roared over and over until the air was dancing with magic. The swirls began to dissolve into tiny, glittering pieces.

Rani gave a satisfied sigh as the first shining droplets landed on the topmost branches of the trees. They balanced there for a moment, sparkling like jewels, before seeping in. More and more magic droplets fell over the forest. As they sank in, the grass became greener, the flowers smelled sweeter, and the lakes were more sparkly. Animals scurried out of their homes, paws and heads and fins raised to the sky to receive the magic rain. It was like the whole forest was being recharged!

As the sun steadily rose, the scent of spring wafted through the air, mixing with the strawberry and lime of the Sky Swirls. A chorus of birdsong rang out, sweet and clear.

"The birds always sing when they get topped up with Sky Swirl energy," Flittercub explained.

"But I've never heard them sing quite that loudly," TrustyPup commented.

"Me neither." Splishi giggled. "They sound almost like they're roaring. There's definitely some Dragon Girl magic blended into the mixture!"

Rani saw a light deep in the forest below, even warmer than the rising sun.

Flittercub, TrustyPup, and Splishi surrounded her. "We must say goodbye now," Flittercub said sadly.

"We'll never forget you." TrustyPup gave Rani a quick lick on the cheek. "You made us feel like real Questies."

"As far as I'm concerned, you ARE real Questies," Rani said, hugging each of the little animals in turn. "I was lucky to have you helping me."

"Will you come back and visit us one day?" Splishi asked, a little shyly.

"I'd love to!" Rani caught the three little creatures up in a hug. "Thanks again, you wonderful friends."

She felt a lump forming in her throat. Before she started crying, Rani tucked in her wings and whooshed lower. The cool morning

air rushed past her and the glade's force field tingled against her scales as she passed through. She skidded to a stop on the glade's grass.

The Tree Queen was already in human form, watching her with a smile. Had some of the Sky Swirl magic seeped into the glade as well? The Tree Queen's leaves looked greener and her brown eyes extra twinkly.

"I will be honest, Enchanted Dragon," the Tree Queen said in her rich voice. "I feared this quest would be impossible. Not only was it extremely challenging, but you had to do it on your own."

"Not on my own," Rani said. "The junior Questies helped me."

The Tree Queen's smile broadened. "And I will be sure to thank them. But even so, I am very grateful for your bravery, Enchanted Dragon."

Rani knew she'd done a good job. She had found the missing Questies, and lifted the spell cast upon them. She had returned the Sky Swirl magic to the forest. She had even reined in the Shadow Queen, just as the Tree Queen had asked.

But there was something she hadn't achieved. "I wanted to bring the Shadow Queen here to speak to you." Rani sighed. "I thought she'd changed, and you two could be close again."

It made Rani sad to think of sisters not speaking to each other.

"You tried your best," the Tree Queen said gently. "Perhaps I shall reach out to her. I have been angry for a long time. Maybe it's time for me to let that go."

Rani suddenly remembered the object the Shadow Queen had left for her sister. "She asked me to give you this." Rani held it out.

The moment the Tree Queen saw the key, her expression changed. Her eyes filled with tears.

"What's wrong?" Rani asked. "Is this something bad?"

The Tree Queen shook her head. "It's not bad, but it's very magical. My sister used it to turn me into a half-tree. Then she took it and hid it. Now . . . well, I could return to my human form."

Rani stood still, waiting for the Tree Queen to take the key. But a few moments passed and the key stayed where it was, on Rani's outstretched paw. "Don't you want to become fully human again?" she asked.

Very slowly, the Tree Queen shook her head. "I don't think I do. My sister's spell gave me powers I wouldn't have otherwise had. My roots reach deep into the earth so I can sense trouble before it grows too big. My leaves reach high into the air, picking up vibrations from far away. Being half-tree connects me to the plants and animals in the Magic Forest. It has made me a better ruler, I am sure of it. All the same, this key is a very important object and must be kept safe. Please bury it in the ground near my roots, Enchanted Dragon."

Rani did so, and as she patted the earth back down, a perfect flower pushed up out of the soil, marking the place.

"The key will be out of harm's way there," the Tree Queen said. "And perhaps a day will come when I need it."

There was another object Rani needed to return. She slipped the guider-scope off, but as she tried to hand it back, the Tree Queen shook her head.

"Keep it," she said. "It will work differently once it's out of the Magic Forest, but it will remind you of your adventures here. Now, take a step forward and I will send you home."

The Tree Queen shook her branches, showering the air with leaves and petals. A gust of wind lifted them, swirling and twirling them around Rani. She closed her eyes as she rose off the ground and started spinning.

Goodbye, Magic Forest, she murmured under her breath. *I hope to see you again someday.*

The spinning slowed and Rani felt the ground beneath her feet once more. She opened her eyes. She was in the backstage area of the theater!

She blinked. Had all that even happened?

She felt like she had just watched the most incredible play. She looked down. Her body had turned back into a girl's. She sighed a little. Being a dragon was cool!

But then Rani saw what was in her hands. The guider-scope! When she held it to her eye, she saw a beautiful forest, glittering in the morning sun. As she watched, three little creatures flew past. A lion cub, a puppy, and a tiny penguin.

"Rani, there you are! We've been looking for you everywhere!" Rani's sister called. "Are you ready to go home?"

Rani dropped the guider-scope and flung her arms around Anjali. She felt like she hadn't seen her sister in weeks. "Anjali, will you miss me when you move out?"

"I'll miss you SO much!" Anjali hugged Rani back. "And don't worry. I was just telling Mom

and Dad that I'll be back every Sunday night, for a home-cooked meal and to do my laundry. And to see you, little sis."

"You'd better," said Rani. "Or I'll..."

Anjali raised one eyebrow, grinning. "Or you'll what?"

A laugh burst from Rani. "Or I'll turn you into a tree!"

Love Dragon Girls?

Turn the page to find out what kind of Dragon Girl you are, learn about the Questies, and more!

What kind of Dragon Girl are you?

Are you a Glitter, Treasure, Night, Sea, or Storm Dragon? Take our quiz to find out!

What word best describes you?

a) Daydreamer

b) Curious

c) Creative

d) Nature-loving

e) Sporty

What do you most love doing on the weekend?

a) Curling up with a book

b) Window-shopping

c) Any craft activity

d) Exploring a nearby forest or park

e) Anything sports-related

What's your favorite subject?

a) Reading and writing

b) Math

c) Art

d) Science

e) Gym

If you could paint your bedroom any color or pattern, what would you choose?

a. Planets and stars

b. Any color, as long as it's bright

c. A mural of your own design

d. Moody swirls and patterns

e. An underwater scene

What's your ideal vacation?

a. Seeing lots of movies

b. Going thrift-store shopping

c. Learning a new style of dance

d. Camping in nature

e. A family hiking trip or bike ride

What's the coolest thing at an amusement park?

a. Haunted house

b. Fortune teller

c. Gift shop

d. Roller coaster

e. Waterslide

DID YOU ANSWER:

MOSTLY As: You'd make a fabulous Night Dragon. You're a daydreamer with a great imagination. You love reading books, watching movies, and stargazing at night!

MOSTLY Bs: Hello there, Treasure Dragon! You are always on the lookout for special things, and have a great eye for finding hidden treasures where no one else can see them. You find the best shells at the beach and that bargain at the thrift store. You love bright colors, jewelry, and secrets.

MOSTLY Cs: You definitely belong with the Glitter Dragons. You are super creative and very artistic. You love dancing, making and listening to music, and are usually working on lots of different craft projects at the same time.

MOSTLY Ds: You'll fit right in with the Storm Dragons. You are super connected to nature, and care deeply about the environment. You love being outside as much as possible—rain, hail, or shine.

MOSTLY Es: We see you, Sea Dragon! You are sporty and full of energy. You're always on the move. You'd much rather run around with friends or go for a swim than sit around chatting. If you see a ball, you want to kick it. Mountains? They're for climbing!

A MIX: You are an Enchanted Dragon! Like Rani, you are multitalented—there's a bit of each dragon in you.

Pop Quiz

How well do you know the Dragon Girls series?

1) Who is Mei's forest helper?

a Buttercub

b LuckyStar

c Squeaklet

2) In *Azmina the Gold Glitter Dragon*, who challenges the Dragon Girls to a flying competition?

a The Glow Bees

b The Shadow Sprites

c The Book Butterflies

3) What type of dragon girl is Zoe?

a Treasure

b Storm

c Sea

4) In *Naomi the Rainbow Glitter Dragon*, we discover Naomi is especially good at what?

a Staying calm

b Solving riddles

c Doing arts and crafts

5) The first Night Dragons book is:

(a) *Stella the Starlight Dragon*

(b) *Phoebe the Moonlight Dragon*

(c) *Rosie the Twilight Dragon*

6) Who calls the girls into the Magic Forest?

(a) The Fire Queen

(b) The little forest helpers

(c) The Tree Queen

Bonus Question!

What treasure does Quinn have to find and return to the vault?

(a) The Heartstring Violin

(b) The Magic Mirror

(c) The Forest Book

Rankings

MINI-FAN (Up to 4 correct):

Lucky you, mini-fan! You've got plenty of Dragon Girls books yet to read!

FAN (4–5 correct):

You've clearly read lots of books in the series. Remember, you're only a book or two away from becoming a super fan. You can do it!

SUPER FAN (6 correct):

The Magic Forest needs readers just like you. You're almost ready to become a Dragon Girl yourself!

DRAGON GIRLS HALL OF FAME (all questions correct; including bonus):

Welcome to the Hall of Fame. Can you hear the Tree Queen cheering your arrival? There are only a few readers in here, so congratulations!

Meet the Questies!

Every Dragon Girl has a special animal friend who helps with her adventure.

Name: Buttercub
Dragon Girl: Azmina the Gold Glitter Dragon
Buttercub has soft golden fur like a lion, yellow spots, and beautiful butterfly wings. He is Flittercub's older brother.

Name: Delphina
Dragon Girl: Willa the Silver Glitter Dragon
Delphina is a gleaming, silver-skinned dolphin who leaves a glittering trail of stars as she flies. Delphina leaps out of the water and does loops in the air like an acrobat training for the circus!

Name: Unichick
Dragon Girl: Naomi the Rainbow Glitter Dragon
Unichick has bright tail feathers, a long pony-like tail, tiny wings that are all colors of the rainbow, and a small unicorn horn atop her forehead. Unichick's feathers glow when she flies!

Name: Squeaklet
Dragon Girl: Mei the Ruby Treasure Dragon
Squeaklet is a pink, fluffy mouse with a pom-pom at the end of his long tail. He can travel through the magic forest by jumping from tree to tree!

Name: PlushyPup
Dragon Girl: Aisha the Sapphire Treasure Dragon
PlushyPup is a dark blue husky puppy with gold markings around his face and wings! He can fly and lives high in the mountains with his family. He is TrustyPup's older brother.

Name: FlutterDash
Dragon Girl: Quinn the Jade Treasure Dragon
FlutterDash is a green owl with a flash of gold under her wings. She is a fast and skilled flyer!

Name: GlidyCat

Dragon Girl: Rosie the Twilight Dragon

GlidyCat has the face and body of a kitten and the wings of a bat. She hangs upside down from tree branches and can swing off of them!

Name: DasherGirl

Dragon Girl: Pheobe the Moonlight Dragon

DasherGirl is a small elk with antlers reaching up from her head and has raccoon markings on her tail. She is swift, darting through the forest and doing midair loops.

Name: LuckyStar

Dragon Girl: Stella the Starlight Dragon

LuckyStar is a golden starfish with a unicorn horn. He does cartwheels in the air!

Name: FinFin

Dragon Girl: Grace the Cove Dragon

FinFin is a small fish with a purple tail, a pink face, and an orange body and fins! She can fly with her fins and even do flips in the air.

Name: Splashi

Dragon Girl: Zoe the Beach Dragon

Splashi is a tiny, pink-and-white pixie penguin with wings. She flies by waddling her whole body and she can even surf! She is Splishi's cousin.

Name: JellyJo

Dragon Girl: Sofia the Lagoon Dragon

JellyJo is a tiny pink jellyfish with friendly eyes and a big smile. She can use her tentacles to twirl in the air like a dancer!

Name: Beebi

Dragon Girl: Hana the Thunder Dragon

Beebi is a fluffy bear cub! He has a low growl and gets around by riding on Hana's back!

Name: Gleami

Dragon Girl: Mina the Lightening Dragon

Gleami is a dragonfly with the face of a dragon. When she laughs, tiny puffs of smoke come out of her nose.

Name: Snowfi

Dragon Girl: Zora the Snow Dragon

Snowfi is a fluffy white fox with tiny wings. She is an expert flyer in cold, snowy conditions.

Name: Flittercub

Dragon Girl: Rani the Enchanted Dragon

Flittercub is a junior Questie with the fur of a lion cub and the wings of a butterfly. She is Buttercub's little sister.

Name: TrustyPup

Dragon Girl: Rani the Enchanted Dragon

TrustyPup is a junior Questie. She is a puppy with wings to help her fly through the air. Her older brother is PlushyPup.

Name: Splishi

Dragon Girl: Rani the Enchanted Dragon

Splishi is a junior Questie. She is a tiny penguin with fluttery wings. Her cousin is Splashi.

Read on for a special sneak peek of

Hana the Thunder Dragon!

Hana blinked, letting her eyes adjust to the gloom. Thunder rolled again. But it sounded different this time. Was it closer or farther away? Hana couldn't tell.

Light filtered through the willow branches.

Except—how odd!—the tree had changed. It was covered in sweet-smelling purple flowers. Surely they hadn't been there a moment ago?

Something strange was going on. The light grew brighter as Hana pushed her way through the leaves. She stopped in surprise. The neat and orderly garden around the banquet hall had vanished. In its place was a wild forest. Tall trees with rough bark stretched toward the sky. The smooth lawn had been replaced by mossy rocks and colorful shrubbery.

A little creature hurried past. The animal looked like a rabbit...but it had a neon-pink tail.

Hana blinked again. *I'll go and find Mina,*

she decided. Her twin would figure out what was going on. Mina was lightning fast at solving mysteries.

Then Hana noticed two things. Two very *impossible* things.

The first was that the entire banquet hall had vanished. There was no sign of it at all!

The second was that her legs had disappeared. Well, not *disappeared* exactly. But they had changed. A lot! Her normal legs had been replaced with powerful limbs covered in gleaming scales. The new shoes Hana's mom had bought her for the party had also vanished. Now her feet were huge paws with sharp claws.

DRAGON GIRLS

#1: Azmina the Gold Glitter Dragon

#2: Willa the Silver Glitter Dragon

#3: Naomi the Rainbow Glitter Dragon

#4: Mei the Ruby Treasure Dragon

#5: Aisha the Sapphire Treasure Dragon

#6: Quinn the Jade Treasure Dragon

#7: Rosie the Twilight Dragon

#8: Phoebe the Moonlight Dragon

#9: Stella the Starlight Dragon

Collect them all!

#10: Grace the Cove Dragon

#11: Zoe the Beach Dragon

#12: Sofia the Lagoon Dragon

#13: Hana the Thunder Dragon

#14: Mina the Lightning Dragon

#15: Zora the Snow Dragon

Special Edition: Rani the Enchanted Dragon

DRAGON GAMES

PLAY THE GAME. SAVE THE REALM.

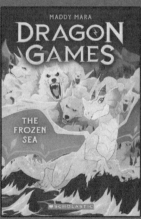

READ ALL OF TEAM DRAGON'S ADVENTURES!

ABOUT THE AUTHORS

Maddy Mara is the pen name of Australian creative duo Hilary Rogers and Meredith Badger. Hilary and Meredith have been making children's books together for many years. They love dreaming up new ideas and always have lots of projects bubbling away. When not writing, Hilary can be found cooking weird things or going on long walks, often with Meredith. And Meredith can be found teaching English online all around the world or daydreaming about being able to fly. They both live on the lands of the Wurundjeri people in Melbourne, Australia. Their website is maddymara.com.